The Ghost of the Fifth Door

The Ghost of the Fifth Door

MARY D. ROBERTS

Illustrated by H. Tom Hall

MACRAE SMITH COMPANY : Philadelphia

For my *NEPHEWS:*
Billy Thursland and Larry Duffy

For my *NIECES:*
Jo Ann Thursland and Barbara Ann Duffy

> *Suddenly ghosts walked*
> *And four doors were five*

MARK VAN DOREN

Contents

1

>>>>>

Work at the Dig

GEORGE LOGO CLIMBED THE GRASSY SLOPE AND
stood for a moment looking down into a valley
studded with olive groves.

"Ajax?" Where was that donkey?

He needed the animal to carry him up into the
hills and over to Salamis to the dig where he
would work for the American archaeologist, Dr.
Craig. If he got there before Char! He searched
the shady path along the riverbank, thinking that
Char Kypou, the Turk, his enemy, needed the
work as badly as he did. Char's parents had been
killed during the 1963 trouble by a Greek bomb
tossed into the truck in which they were riding.

Char now had only his grandmother and he needed to work to help her.

George's dark eyes searched the shady path along the riverbank once again. He and Char had been friends until Cyprus was divided between Greek and Turk. A green line now separated their villages. To cross over that line would be flirting with death from a stray bullet.

George decided to take the short, but dangerous, route to Salamis but he wanted to save time. To lose a friend because of war was bad enough; to lose an important job to an enemy would make him the laughingstock of his village. It wasn't only the money. He was interested in archaeology and had spent all the time he could in the past two summers at the site. Now, he had the chance of being paid for doing the work he liked best.

Startled by the donkey's braying, George leaped into the air.

Ajax was near the edge of the sea where the sealed wall of Kyrenia Castle touched shore. George ran to him, grabbed the rope on the donkey's halter and yanked, scolding, "It's as my mother says; you are a worthless no-good." He added, for good measure, "Also, you eat too much."

At the village fountain, George ran cold water over his face, neck and hair, then gave Ajax a cool drink from a tin can. He patted the animal between its ears, as they trudged to Salamis. The road was hot and dusty; the gorge green and full of the sound of rushing water; in the air was the scent of lemon blossoms, the perfume of Cyprus.

George left the animal in the shade of a tree and ran toward the boom-town of tents. Inside the main tent, he searched his pocket for the permit from the Cyprus Department of Antiquity but, before he could hand it to Dr. Craig, Char, it seemed, from out of nowhere, grabbed the permit out of his hand, insisting, "I was here first."

Losing his balance from the shove, George landed in the sand on his belly, one hand covering his eyes and the other his left ear. He grabbed Char's leg and pulled him down to the ground and rubbed his face in the sand until Dr. Craig interrupted the free-for-all, saying, "I know how important this job is to both of you. Look, I'll put you both on the payroll, but you'll be on trial for two weeks." The broad-shouldered man shook hands with each boy; his black hair almost touched the top of the canvas tent.

"Fair enough." George said.

Dr. Craig shook his head. "If only the budget would allow, I'd keep both of you for the summer."

George worked that morning with Kathy Craig, the professor's thirteen-year-old daughter. "Howdy, kiddo," he called, walking from his hips, trying to imitate an American cowboy. "How's tricks?"

"Hi, George," she said, happy to see him.

Kathy, blonde and tall for her age, loved adventure and reading. If she wasn't acting out an adventure, she was reading about one. An ideal world, to her, would be where people rode elephants down Main Street instead of buses. Happy as a lark, she didn't know the meaning of the word *trouble!*

Following Dr. Craig's directions, George picked up a trowel and started to dig a pit about ten inches deep, making sure to keep the sides neat and straight. Char walked by on his way to the east end of the dig where the Turks worked. He gave Kathy a friendly wave and the brightest of smiles, but scowled at George.

"I don't see why you and Char can't be friends again," Kathy said, truly puzzled. "Before you were born, could you decide whether you would be born a Greek or a Turk?"

Now George was puzzled. If only he could once again say to Char "Sit down with me and share everything I have," as they once did. Yet he knew, no matter how much he might want to be friends, it couldn't be.

Impatiently, he kicked the sand with his heel, thinking of how he couldn't explain all this to Kathy, who was a free and happy American.

Kathy lifted her pith helmet with an ice pick, saying, "If only we could find something very important. All I got yesterday was pottery, fragments of roof tiles."

George wrapped a kerchief around his forehead to keep the sweat out of his eyes. "Something, maybe, as important as the treasure hidden by the ghost of the fifth door?" He thumped his chest. "Zoume!" He measured his nose with two fingers. "I was this close to the fifth door this morning."

Kathy looked at him sideways. "No one can get that close to the inner castle. There is the twenty-foot wall blockade, you know."

"True," he answered, goodnaturedly. "And a United Nations Patrol is always on guard, near

14

the wall. These days one can get shot for being too nosey."

"Someday I'm going over that wall," Kathy said firmly.

"Ha, there would not be a freckle left to you."

George explained how the Venetians had built a massive twenty-foot wall around the inner medieval castle. Beyond the wall, there was a drawbridge connecting the wall to the castle, but it had been locked since the time of the Crusades. According to legend, there was also a secret entrance, not yet found by anyone.

Kathy protested. "Strong swimmers have circled that wall many times and found no opening, only cracks that a hand couldn't fit into."

George shrugged. "The Venetians hid their treasures in the castle until their ships set sail for Venice. They had to have some means of going in and out."

She nodded.

Five delta-shaped doors of iron hugged the inner castle, two to the right of the drawbridge, two on the left, and one directly facing it. This was the fifth door! No one knew the secret, either, of how these doors opened. It was believed that behind the iron doors were armour-clad skeletons from the time of the Crusades, and that four skulls turned toward the fifth door in the wall— sentries to a ghost so terrifying it was synonymous with the evil eye. "Last week a soldier tried to hammer at every crevice in the wall and fell into the ocean and drowned." George shook his head slowly. "The ghost killed him before he could discover the secret entrance."

"That doesn't compute." Kathy used her favorite expression for things that didn't add up. "Maybe I don't believe in ghosts."

George thought this over. "Well, sitting here in daylight with people all around, I could say there is no ghost of the fifth door. He has no face, he doesn't eat or sleep. Yet, when I'm alone and it's dark, I believe that he's in the castle."

"I know what you mean," Kathy said. "When I read a book, I'm always the heroine and I do exciting things and solve big and dangerous problems, but in real life, if someone says something mean about me in school, I'm not brave. I just feel like crying."

The sun grew hotter and it was more comfortable to talk than work on pottery. Kathy told George about a ghost she had seen, stateside, on TV. "Real horrible!"

"What's TV?" George asked, then listened closely as she explained.

Kathy sketched a TV set in the sand; George studied the drawing. "There are machines like that in the big hotels in Nicosia." He laughed hard. "The people in it are so small, how can they scare anyone?"

"George," she pulled on his hair, "you're a donkey."

George wriggled his ears and brayed like a donkey until Kathy was in hysterics.

No one worked during the midday meal that lasted for two hours. George fed and watered Ajax. Over a brushwood fire he heated rice and lamb wrapped in vine leaves. For dessert, handfuls of black, green and white grapes that his mother had given him were shared with Kathy, who, in turn, shared with Char. The rocky slopes of the valley seemed to hold all the heat in the world. The valley was treeless except for a crooked column of Judas trees.

George slept against an olive tree until Ahmed, the foreman of diggers, woke him shouting: "Did the prophet not say 'an honest day's work for an honest day's pay'?"

By evening a section of about a quarter of an

17

acre was dug; groups of workers sifted the earth in this section while others were engaged in a new cut on the southerly side. The whistle blew; work stopped. Ahmed shouted. "Now you've earned some rest." He was a hawk-nosed swarthy man who always wore dirty trousers but brilliantly colored clean shirts.

They went home to Kyrenia among donkeys and dusty lorries. Traffic lessened down each ridge of the road, and for the final quarter mile to Kyrenia George was the only traveler from the Nicosia crossroads. A small flock of sheep grazed in a field on the left of the hill; a screeching bird and a sheep's bell ringing broke the silence. The village coffeehouse was as silent as a tomb behind closed shutters. George rode by the shop and came to the end of the narrow street. He found himself on the riverbank facing the haunted castle of Kyrenia that had once been a stronghold, centuries ago, of the English king, Richard the Lionhearted.

The ghost had been a crusader who had died in the castle. It was his skeleton, legend claimed, that stood dressed in armour behind the delta, the fifth door. The last time the ghost had left the castle had been two decades ago when the most priceless antiquity in the world of the Middle East had been stolen. The Mycenaen golden-winged horse had never been recovered. Oh, for the courage to go into the castle and seek the treasure. It had to be there, for didn't legend also claim that the ghostly knight, vexed with men's greed for gold, had taken the golden-winged horse back with him, into the castle? Others believed that the treasure was not in the castle, but that the thieves who had stolen it, wished to put the blame on the ghostly knight. George, as he rode along, sang the question song that he and Kathy had made up last summer:

How many miles to go to find a treasure?
A hundred and ten?
Well then—only a hundred and ten
If you can go there—and come back again.

2

>>>>>

Uncle Spiros's Secret

IN GEORGE'S VILLAGE HENS SCRATCHED IN THE DUST
under fig trees, and a pitiless sun beat on the
unpaved square, but the whitewashed cottages
of Kyrenia were surrounded by orchards and
overhanging vines. The Logo house stood by itself at the end of the lane that led to the harbor
via a steep rock path of hundreds of wobbly rocks.
George's father, a fisherman, kept his boat at
the end of the harbor basin. In the garden, flow-
ers grew everywhere, and beside paths around
the house. George turned the corner and was
startled to hear his mother crying.

"Ma-ma?"

She sat just inside the door of her cottage. A sea breeze ruffled a slip of black hair that crept out from her many hairpins. Mrs. Logo wiped away her tears with the corner of her white apron. "Uncle Spiros—his hours are ending." The priest had brought word that afternoon.

The last wish of his great-uncle was that George come to his village right away, as the dying man had something to say for George's ears alone. George did not wait for supper, but left the house right away. Seeing that his father's boat was nowhere on the horizon, George would go overhill to Troodos, and beyond that to the village of St. George, where Uncle Spiros had lived for eighty years. On the dusty road George scattered chickens out of his way, turned to the right, then made his way ascending the edge of the cliff. It was dangerous crawling; the bank had been eaten away by the last earthquake. It was a starless night; one step out of turn or to trip would land him in a river of rocks and his head would be crushed like an egg. A quarter of a mile up, an underfed dog darted like a sharp shadow in front of him, scaring him to the bottom of his wits. The dog's bark made him less nervous.

24

He hadn't too far to go now, and this thought made him feel safer.

Then, his self-confidence gone, he stood shaking at the sight before him. Lit by the moon there stood what must be a ghost; it was so thin, so tall, and whitefaced. The spectre stretched out its long arms wildly and moved as if swayed by music. A low fire held in a cup of earth glowed in the distance. But—it was no ghost, for the shadow carried a rifle and as he neared the firelight, George could see that he was dressed like a patchwork scarecrow: red bandana, khaki jacket, English or American pants, and, to George's relief, he sang suddenly and loudly—and in Greek. George grinned happily and approached the stranger. "I thought you were a ghost or a Turkish sentry."

The man on guard duty for his village was also happy, "I am glad you are not a Turk. I don't ever want to have to kill."

They chatted for a few seconds and then George hurried on up the seldom-used path that was not even suitable for donkeys; it was that wild and craggy, and the faint grass that grew in dark patches was not fit for even mountain goats.

To the south the path was easier. The thought

of his uncle gave him fresh courage and he ran on, but too quickly, for he slipped and fell on a scraggly bush and the dust rose in swift clouds, like a small atomic explosion. None the worse, except for a few scratches and a torn tee shirt, he hurried along, almost running, until he reached the bridge that crossed the stream to the village of St. George. The village itself was still invisible beneath the starless sky, and soundless except for the slop of water and the plop now and again of a frog diving into the stream.

Within the village was an avenue of lemon trees and beyond the lemon trees, the house of Spiros. The grinding of a key in a rusted lock and the wooden door that opened into the cottage staggered on its hinges, then flew open. In a voice as soft as putty, his uncle whispered, "I have sent everyone away so that I can talk to you whom I have looked upon as a son."

"Are you in pain, uncle?"

"Every living thing suffers pain. Has the war not taught you that?"

A long silence. Then Spiros raised a bony hand slowly and moved it toward the edge of the cot and tapped on the wooden board. "Remove the board."

27

George was surprised—the solid wood seemed to be part of the bed. He pushed and tugged at the board, then finding that the nails were rusted into the mahogany, he took a long time to loosen these. "There's nothing under here," he told his uncle finally.

Spiros tapped his shoulder and pointed to a long, scarred coffee table in a corner to the right of a shabby sofa. On the table was a candle. George lit this and looked again. Under the bed was a velvet cloth.

"Raise the cloth," Spiros commanded.

Empty space, but at a point underneath the rusted spring was a cord of black, red, and yellow threads. George tugged the cord and—gasped!

"It's been there and on my conscience for twenty years," said Spiros.

George looked at the treasure, then held it in both hands to feel its weight, smell its metallic odor and hear the resounding click as he scraped a fingernail against its base. He tasted in his heart the joy of knowing that he would share in the reward. Then his own conscience asked him what right his uncle had to this treasure.

Spiros the shepherd told the story of how he, and not the ghost of the fifth door, came by the

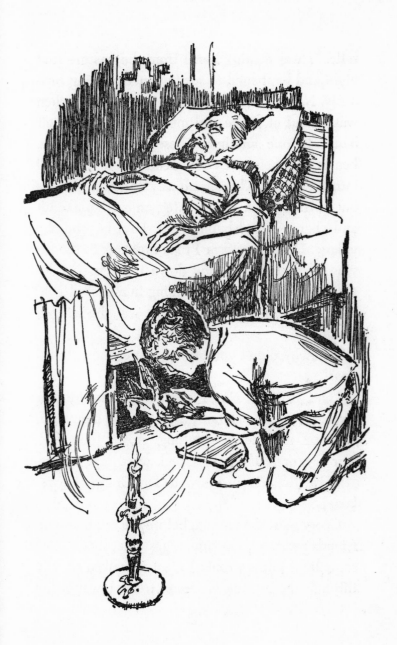

relic. "I was coming home from the pasture that night and happened to see two men arguing furiously. Now it's a common sight, but Cyprus then was a land of peace and men did not raise their hands to one another. These men fought like beasts and before I could reach them they fell into the ravine. There is no way of getting bodies out of the ravine. Weeks later, an earthquake hit and changed the shape of this land beyond the village. During a storm I took my flock to the ravine pasture and looking down I saw two skeletons and, beside one, swimming in a mist of gold that looked like spangled tissue, was the winged horse."

"But why didn't you turn it over to the authorities?"

"The British? No, I recognize only Mother Greece." Weak as he was, he said the word, "Greece" as if he were calling "*Aera*," the Greek war cry, or "*Nike*," the Greek word for Victory.

"Give the treasure now to Dr. Craig." He relaxed.

George left the cottage before the relatives and friends returned. Outside, a gossamer moon gave some light to the evening. George walked rapidly through the avenue of lemon trees, towards the ravine that twisted up into the flank of the Troodos Mountains. It was far easier going downhill. His uncle had warned that even the walls of Cyprus had eyes and ears, and that George was to speak to no one until the treasure was in Dr. Craig's hands.

That couldn't be soon enough for George.

He stopped to drink from the spring beneath the bridge. There was a face in the water and it was not his own. It was the reflection of someone's head watching him from the bridge. No doubt a shepherd. He washed the dust from his hands and face, feeling secure when the reflection had disappeared. He walked on but knew he must not walk too quickly by the coffeehouse, for in a country like Cyprus, to hurry was to cast suspicion upon oneself.

When a shadow dropped across his path, he knew he was being followed; there was a rattle of pebbles, then the scrape of a foot.

A stranger stood in the path with a knife clutched in his right hand. Half under his breath, in a curse and a threat, he demanded the treasure. George kicked him in the shin and there was a clatter on the stones as he dropped the knife. George ran as fast as he could up the rocky terrain of the ravine, and didn't stop until he came to a familiar place: the shepherd's hut. The hut, usually clean and tidy, was now filthy.

When he opened the battered wooden door, stench, dust and flying insects greeted him from the dark interior. The pale moonlight at his back lit up the hut; rough bedding lay in a corner, and beside this, dried shrubs or ferns that had probably served as a mattress.

Too late he realized that the stranger had been living here waiting for Spiros to die. George had walked into a deliberate trap. He fell to the ground as a bullet whizzed by his ear, missing him by a fraction. After a few moments he crawled, then he ran.

He was running down the dark lane under a starless sky, clutching the velvet-wrapped relic to his chest. He didn't lessen his pace until he reached home, where the only sound he heard was that of snoring. He crept into the house, trying to think of the best place to hide the golden-winged horse. He then slipped into the pantry where onions, made into ropes, and braided together by their tops, hung beside strings of peppers of red, green and mixed colors. The longest rows of all were the salted fish and on cool shelves in a dark corner were stacks of

Cyprus cheese. He placed the antique carefully behind one of the stacks, then sighed with relief.

Before the war, his parents had always put their big iron bed outside the house, under the largest tree in the arbor, and had slept there each night during the summer until September when the first rains came. Now, with all the trouble on the island, it would be too dangerous, and they slept inside during the hot weather. George stood for a moment in the doorway of his parents' bedroom. His mother, in her white nightgown, was as plump as a full moon. The snores of his father were as loud as a brass band. Yet, George heard footsteps. The stranger was coming after him. He turned in the doorway and saw under massive brows dark eyes as searching and as sharp as a wolf's. George yelled his head off. "The ghost! The ghost!"

"What? What?" his father leaped out of bed, then ran around the house searching, and when he found no one, he became very angry with George. "This has happened before. The other time you went to the castle at night and saw a tiger on the wall. Every man in the village hurried down there with a hoe. It was a tiger, all right. A tiger cat—only two hands big."

George had been sorry about that. "Ba-ba, this is much different." He started to explain about the winged horse.

"Go to bed," his father roared like a lion. "And leave the ghosts of Cyprus in peace. And me, too," he added, crawling back into bed.

His mother said, with a quick, fading smile, "Be careful, my son, the night opens and closes like a coffin when you try to solve the mystery of a ghost."

He went to bed as he was told. It was best, perhaps, to tell them of the golden-winged horse in the morning. The stranger could be nearby and listening now.

But he tossed and turned so much, he was forced to get out of bed and creep back to his parents. George whispered the story to them of how Spiros had come by the relic; how someone had tried tonight, to take it away from him; and of how he had run with it, clutched inside his shirt. George told them everything.

His father, still half-asleep, growled, "You have told us what you must. The antique is safe. Now go to sleep. In the morning, we'll talk more."

Suddenly realizing how hungry he was, George went to the pantry and ate a large cheese pie. But he did not return to his cot to sleep; instead, he sat down in a corner of the pantry, folded his arms and crossed his legs, and didn't even close his eyes. He was a sentry protecting a valuable treasure.

3

>>>>>

To Catch a Thief

GEORGE WOKE TO THE SMELL OF SIZZLING SAUSAGES and scrambled eggs. He greeted his mother and sat at the table, anxious to tell more about the treasure, but his mother was adjusting the primus stove and couldn't be disturbed. Mr. Logo, although a young man still, had as many lines on his face as a fishing net. Because he was poor, his favorite expression was, "Money is the beauty of a man in the eyes of the world." He had black brows that arched above merry eyes and he wasn't a true cynic. He pounded George on the back in farewell, and went to his boat, saying, "Do as Spiros said. Only Dr. Craig will really know if it

is the treasure. Here are some piasters. Take the bus. You'll be safe."

As George walked along the road to the bus, the hot dust picked at him like sandpaper. The wall of the castle, under the blinding sun, looked like granulated sugar that might melt in seconds; yet centuries had seen that wall. The sky was as deep a blue as the sun was red. At 6:30, the bus stopped at the village fountain. The only empty seat was beside Char. George sat down and folded his arms; neither boy greeted the other. Greeks spoke only to other Greeks and Turks to Turks. The bus headed for Nicosia, the capital. Muslim women hidden by veils, like tiny potato sacks, sat patient and concealed in the back of the bus.

Metaxis Square was a hot oven and a human ocean that roared like a seashell pressed against one's ear. People shrieked, strove, rang bicycle bells and auto horns, swore at donkeys, pommelled one another in friendship, recited the *Koran,* argued or bargained: all with frenzy. After Nicosia, there were vacant seats; George sat alone by the window. United Nations flags flew everywhere; Danes patroled in jeeps, while Finnish soldiers whizzed along Kyrenia road on motorcycles. From the minaret of the mosque of St. Sophia, a muzzein called Muslims to prayer. The bus edged along Ledra Street, a crooked, narrow thoroughfare where policemen stood guard, as well as soldiers of the UN peace-keeping force. They marched in twos and threes and looked proud under their blue berets.

Near the open fields, George leaned out the paneless window and greeted an old man, bent over a hoe, his legs curved inside black pantaloons and boots. He raised his square bushy head and returned the greeting: "Rejoice in this day!"

The camp was pitched beyond the city in the green plain that lies between Salamis and the sea. Dr. Craig was in front of the main tent wearing sunglasses, an old yacht cap, starched khaki trousers. He held a towel over his arm, looking pleased with himself; a confident, strong man, he stood by the tent with the air of someone who had enough know-how to think and do what needed to be done, always.

Proudly George unrolled the velvet cloth and presented the golden horse to Dr. Craig. Once inside the tent he told the startled archaeologist the complete story.

"For the first time in my life, I'm at a loss for words," Dr. Craig said, patting the crown of his head. "When I left Philadelphia I never dreamed of finding anything like this." Rewrapping the treasure in its cloth, he added, "I must speak with your uncle at once." He ushered George toward the jeep.

The jeep gathered momentum and proceeded slowly up the dirt road, bumping over ruts of hard mud, until finally, a myriad of foothills beyond, they entered Agios Georgios, the village of St. George. Too late! Spiros had died. Dr. Craig, after offering his sympathies, let George remain to comfort his parents.

George returned to the dig next morning to find policemen and investigators inside the main tent. Kathy told him that the golden-winged horse had been stolen.

"*Oki,* no, how can that be?"

Kathy couldn't answer. Nothing seemed to compute that morning.

Again, Dr. Craig told his story. "I was not dreaming or dozing," he insisted for the nth time, "but writing up a dig report." He shook his head sadly, the twinkle gone from his eyes. He studied the letter, based on his report, that he was sending to the foundation, and grunted. "Someone came in and stole the antique."

"What did he look like?"

"He had a face, or mask, like someone playing the part of a ghost," Dr. Craig answered, "and stood as if he were a connecting link between two worlds. His trench coat fit him like skin."

"He spoke?" the inspector asked.

"As he picked up the golden horse, he said, 'I'll take this.'"

"Was he British, American, or any other foreigner?"

"He spoke slowly and deliberately as if to give the impression he was disguising his voice."

Outside, the police found no trace of anyone who shouldn't be in the camp. Not a single clue. Not even a footprint in the sand. The inspector wrote for a few minutes in a small black book, then said, "I must ask you to come to the Department of Antiquities." Bidding everyone good-by, he left with Dr. Craig by his side.

"This is the work of the ghost," George whispered to Kathy, and told her of how he had followed him home the other night.

Char, forgetting that he was speaking to an enemy, said, "To think that the ghost of the fifth door would steal."

George and Kathy nodded in complete agreement.

Who on the Island of Cyprus could disappear into thin air, except the ghost of the fifth door? Who else could have known that Uncle Spiros had hidden the golden-winged horse for all those years?

Dr. Kazanzi was left in charge of the dig for the remainder of the day and everyone returned to work. The more George thought about it, the more angry he became. His great-uncle had protected the golden-winged horse; then, in a split second, it had been stolen.

Kathy, very determined, said, "I want to find the golden-winged horse and bring it back here. I'm not scared of any ghost who steals." She was so angry she was almost crying. She took a large white sheet of cardboard, red paint and a brush and printed a message. "I want this recopied in Greek and Turkish."

"And Arabic," George advised, holding the cardboard steady.

Later, they watched as an Arab worker ran in a country where even to hurry is to appear unusual, even suspect. Usually a quiet gray-haired thoughtful man, the Arab, very kind to those who worked under him, wore a green band around his fez, showing him to be a Hajji who had been to Mecca. He murmured under his breath, "To catch a thief," then hung up one of the posters.

ONE THOUSAND PIASTERS

For information leading to the arrest and conviction of a person, or persons, who stole a golden-winged horse, a priceless ancient relic, from the Salamis Dig.

Char whistled, then said, "I'd be a Cyprus millionaire with money like that."

George agreed with him. With part of that money, he could buy a real stove for his mother, like those the English and American ladies used. And think, just think, of all the other things he could do, with that kind of money.

Char spoke quickly, and to Kathy. "We Turks have great courage. I could fight a ghost, to make my grandmother rich." To prove he could meet the danger, Char contented himself with drawing a forefinger across his throat and uttering a sinister noise. "Was I born a sheep, or a Turk?" he asked himself, as much as he asked the others.

Although George had the courage of Char,

he was a little less sure. He remembered a young, handsome cousin of his mother's who had dropped dead in the field, mumbling that he had seen the ghost of the fifth door. George shook his head, slightly nervous where the ghost was concerned, as the sun vanished beneath the sea and darkness fell.

Instead of going home to Kyrenia when work had ended for the day, George met his mother at the village of St. George. She had spent the entire day cleaning the house that had belonged to Spiros. Everything in order, she now sat in the rocker, waving the lovely fan that Kathy had given her for all the wonderful grapes at lunchtime. "It is warm, so warm," she said.

Before leaving for home, George closed and locked the four window shutters. The house would remain vacant for several weeks; then, since it had been left as a dowry for a poor female relative, it would be occupied following her marriage, after a short period of mourning.

4

>>>>>

To Catch a Ghost

GEORGE AWOKE NEXT MORNING AND PEEKED OUT
the shutter. It was a brilliant day. He looked from
the balcony to the dirt road. Then, squinting
against the hot sun, he made up his mind that
nothing would stop him in trying to get back the
treasure. It was not only the reward money; family honor was at stake. No matter how scared he
might be, he'd not give up the search. "I couldn't
care less about the ghost or evil eye," he vowed,
keeping a straight face, yet knowing the greater
the lie, the straighter the face.

On the bus he and Char exchanged greetings
by saying, "Clouds are clouds, mountains are

47

mountains." They spoke no more for the rest of the trip. They were by no means friends again, nor were they enemies.

Hermes Christos took George to task for his slowness in digging that day. "Our work is not only finding great treasures," he yelled, towering over George. The foreman was so fat, his muscles were like putty. He couldn't sit in a canvas chair, but rested against a tree like an elephant as he delivered his lecture, and his voice was like a speedometer purring off the miles. "We are digging up a city. That means not only treasure but pottery, the everyday things—the four walls that enclosed a home—the tools these ancients tilled the earth with—the pots they cooked in. These, too, are cherished possessions. Now, dig for these," he ordered. "That is what you are being paid for."

George worked for all he was worth, breathing in hot, choking yellow dust. The other diggers shouted as if they wanted to murder one another, but were all really fast friends. The whistle blew and the foreman greeted George with a warm smile and an outstretched hand. "Now you've put in a good day's work."

After work, George hurried to the stream and slipped under the water. He swam out to help his father pull the boat ashore. "Good catch, Ba-ba?"

Deno Logo spit, then scratched the back of his neck. "Nothing." He kicked the boat. A melancholy man, his smile was always weary. He spoke in a thin voice. "Fishing is a bad business when it must be done for a living."

As they walked together George told his father of his plans to get back the treasure. The houses of Kyrenia looked like white ice cubes in the twilight. "Do you know how to catch a ghost?"

Mr. Logo laughed. "I do not even know how to catch fish, and I'm a fisherman."

George knew that his father was the finest fisherman around, but since the hostilities, with all the shooting and the harbor continuously being visited by warships, the fish took refuge in deeper waters.

As George and his father entered the house they touched a talisman of goats' horns nailed to the front door to keep out the evil eye.

"Eat well," his mother said. "You need lots of food to work under a scorching sun all day." She carried a heavy tray of baked fish to the table, then brought a huge bowl of salad, black olives and fresh bread.

As his mother sipped Turkish coffee in the ar-

49

bor with neighbor women, George's father, his face shining like polished walnut, invited George to the coffeehouse down at the square, for the first time since George had become a teen-ager. George was now a man who could go with other men when work and dinner were over, and talk about all the problems of this and the next world.

The eyes of the village, like the eyes of a cat, began to flame in the night as people lit candles and kerosene lamps, or turned on the electric lights in two or three homes. Outside the coffeehouse most of the men sat at tables. George sipped a coke and listened as his father settled a dispute between two men who were arguing as to why the fish were not biting. "It's the fault of the Americans and their atom bombs." The other, with clenched fist, insisted, "It's the Russians."

Deno Logo added, "It is maybe us. We fish the same as our grandfathers fished." He shrugged. "Fish, like kids today, are too smart. You need modern ways to deal with them."

An angry farmer shouted, "Your ideas would turn Mother Cyprus into a big factory."

"I'm talking about a little change for better living. What need has Cyprus of factories—to export fools like you? Shut your mouth."

The argument ended.

George wasn't too interested in the discussion. At midnight he intended to go to the castle wall. He whistled for courage, thinking: sticks and stones can break my bones, but spooks and ghosts and shadows can only shiver me. Yet, when the church bell struck twelve, he shivered enough to jump out of his skin, though it was a very warm night.

The stars hung over the sand dunes of Kyrenia cove, as if they were rewards for a good drawing. The village slept, except for George. He climbed to the top of the wall to see if there was any other way of getting into the castle, other than through the delta-shaped door, a narrow opening in the lower castle wall. He felt more secure when the UN sentry left his beach patrol and went to the Yacht Club. George brushed lizards out of his way as he crawled like a black fly along the parapet.

The night became a wall of purple to his light-accustomed eyes. There was no sight nor sound of anyone, only the slap of the Mediterranean against the lower castle wall. At this point, worn out with emotion, George fell asleep on the parapet, snuggled securely against a turret.

A strange noise startled him from his sound sleep. It was a jiggling of chains inside the wall— a noise as weird as a dance of death. He caught his breath, then sat up, braced his arm in an iron ring and eased down the rampart, and onto the pier. If only he had brought along a rope, it would have helped his escape. He stepped on a large crab and the torn shell cut his foot. He let out a yell. The rattling of chains stopped.

More startled at the silence than he had been at the noise, George ran up the beach, only to trip and fall as something caught at his foot. Head over heels he fell in the sand and saw stars. When he picked up what he had fallen over, he found that his foot had become trapped in the pocket of a trench coat. He picked it up, rolled it up like a football and dashed home with it under his arm.

At the camp next morning he showed the coat to Dr. Craig and Kathy.

"Dad, it's your coat. Look—an American union label."

Dr. Craig agreed. "The top button is missing." He opened the top drawer of his desk and found a button that matched the others on the coat. "Since it doesn't rain here all summer, I hung this in the photography tent. Who buried it on Kyrenia beach—and why?"

George and Kathy worked all day in air that had been French-fried in humidity. "Whoever the thief is," Kathy said, "he sure seems to have the power of a ghost."

George was also filled with wonder and curiosity. Was this a creature that could hide, at will, under a parapet? Could it change into a lizard? Would they ever see, much less find, the golden-winged horse again?

In his entire life George had never dealt with anything more mysterious than the house sprites with pointed ears who were responsible for turning milk sour, or causing eggs to smash on the floor, and making shutters go boom in the night, sometimes even when they were tightly closed. Now, he was dealing with the shifty, crafty, clever ghost of the fifth door.

Momentarily, the ghost was forgotten as George thought of tomorrow's excursion with Dr. Craig and Char. They would go in the jeep to Nicosia, the metropolis, to the bank on business, and to foodshops for provisions, and to the garage.

5
>>>>>
A Real Arab?

THE BANK HAD BEEN COOL AND DARK AND MUSTY; typewriters clicked in the background. Outside, the square was sunny and full of swirling dust. George and Dr. Craig passed the shish-ke-bab stands that lined the avenue, their odors more pleasing than all the perfume of Arabia. While the jeep was being serviced at the garage of Torikian, next to the tanners where the stink of hide flesh spilled into the street, they hurried around the corner and had lunch.

The ancient, narrow streets of Ataturk Square were so congested, Dr. Craig wiped his brow and

said, "This place makes Times Square seem like a country crossroads."

When they had finished shopping at the market, George boasted, "I bargained so good, I bet I saved you lots of money, hah?"

"Now that's what I call businesslike," Dr. Craig said, approvingly.

Suddenly cold panic clutched at George's heart, and he didn't know why. Was it that Arab moving up the narrow dark alley, turning his head, to the right, then quickly to the left, with half-closed eyes, and chanting in Arabic? An Arab and yet not an Arab? His fingers slipped idly over the worry beads he held, but the clicking seemed to have a definite rhythm, like a plea in International Morse Code, not the prayers to Allah that a true Muslim would utter.

Yet he was only one of many Arabs on the streets and alleys of Nicosia, dressed in ragged tunics and striped, faded robes. Except for his tattered red scarf, the worse for wear, he was no different from the others. George put the man out of his mind and got into the jeep beside Dr. Craig. They waited for Char, who had been sent to shop in the Turkish quarter.

When Char joined them, they drove off, then

stopped outside Nicosia near the American Coca-Cola factory. As they sipped cokes outside a restaurant, Dr. Craig said, "Char, I've always wanted to visit a mosque. This seems a good time."

Char directed him to the Mosque of the Companion of the Prophet which was within walking distance. Outside the mosque, they all removed their shoes before entering the house of worship. The low, domed building had oriental carpets that lay thick in splendor, although sections were threadbare. Squatting under oil lamps, they listened to words from the *Koran:*

> *For every nation there is an appointed time.*
> *When their time cometh*
> *Then they cannot put it off one hour*
> *Nor hasten it—*

Char translated the chant from the Turkish to English. Driving home, they all were silent; it had been a very busy and a very interesting day.

Dinner that evening, at the Logo house, was a feast. The table in the arbor was spread with lamb and beans, veal pilaf, ice cold cokes, plus cold drinks of Cyprus, and George's favorite, *kokoretsi* (pieces of meat wrapped tightly in lamb and broiled over charcoal).

Mr. Logo shook hands several times with Dr.

Craig, and insisted that he test all three chairs in the living room to find the one most comfortable.

Mrs. Logo brought the wine and cheese, saying, *"Kopiaste,"* (sit down and share our food).

"Kopiaste!" Mr. Logo repeated the welcome.

George felt sad because Char was absent. How many times Char had feasted with them, and he with Char's family. Now the war had put all that in the past. "What was that word your father just said?" he asked Kathy.

"Ser-en-dip-ity," she answered. "Used to describe the accidental discovery of valuable things by people searching for something else."

"Like the golden-winged horse?"

"Professor," Mr. Logo joked, "you Americans have made so much progress at Salamis, you have about dug yourself out of a job."

"Archaeology is here to stay in Cyprus. There's far more treasure under this earth than on." Dr. Craig added thoughtfully, "The Middle East has cities buried under a sea of sand. Crete had ninety cities, Homer claimed. To date, only seven or eight have been uncovered."

"Ba-ba, Kathy and I unearthed a huge vessel— in good shape still—except for a broken base and small rents in the belly of the bowl. Tomorrow we will chip at the plaster with orange sticks and

dental instruments to restore the mosaic pattern."
George glowed. "How I will like that work,
Ba-ba."

"Hello, hello," someone called, and Sophia, the
jolly wife of the schoolmaster, came puffing to the
table, her apron lumpy with a huge watermelon.
She enfolded Kathy inside her elephantine arms
and wished her a long, happy life with the words:
"eutykhos ti humon anastasi."

The following morning, watching early dawn
begin at Kyrenia Harbor from the wooden shutter, George dressed quickly. In the courtyard a
pleasant surprise: For once Ajax was where he
was supposed to be and had not run off. But all
was not well. The donkey was ill. A rusted nail
had lodged in his right forefoot. George removed
it as gently as he could, then rinsed the paw in
strong soap and steaming water, as his mother
wagged her head in sympathy, uttering, "po-po-
po."

Caring for Ajax caused George to miss his bus;
he was forced to take the secret passage, as dangerous as it was, to Salamis. First, a quarter-mile
swim, then, at the spot where the rock-filled river
and giant crags with tortuous caves cut off sky
and light, he climbed upward slowly, cautiously,
like a cat over slippery boulders, hanging at times

by his fingers and toes to avoid the cascading water. The most dangerous area was at the waterfall beside the spring. The waterfall, a mossy, soft, silver cover of mist, meant he was halfway to the dig, but moss-covered stones lay beneath the water and one slip of one toe would send him crashing against the rocks. He stood on the ledge of rock to dive into the stream and slipped. He clutched a strong vine to break his fall, and when he realized that he had almost broken every bone in his body, he sat down on the boulder, quietly, until his heart stopped pounding.

George then dove into the spring and glided through the water until he came up on the beach. Marble columns stood beside aqueducts that led to circular sunken baths of old Byzantine structures. A slope divided shore from sea. The arid heat dried him, even his hair, in seconds, making him feel as if a hot, dusty towel was being slapped across his body. He had more swimming to do, and did it, before reaching the dig. Once again on the beach, he ignored the heat and rushed to the main tent.

Inside the tent, Dr. Craig rearranged papers on his crate-like desk and looked up, startled. "You crept up on me, George. Everything okay?"

"I'm a little late because Ajax is ill." He told

him about his pet's infected foot. "He is more than a pet," George said, "Ajax is my friend. I almost cannot bear to see him suffer."

Dr. Craig opened a medical kit and handed George a plastic vial, saying "Soak the foot every four hours in this antibiotic. If the infection doesn't clear in a day or two, we'll try something stronger."

George thanked him many times.

"All that matters," Dr. Craig said, "is that the animal get well."

George worked with Kathy through the morning, and in the afternoon they counted pieces of vases that had been cracked by centuries of earthquakes and rejoiced when one black and red figured vase of the sixth century was fully reconstructed.

A digger brought half a brick from the south ditch to the main tent. Was it a relic? Dr. Craig put it to the test by dipping a corner of the brick into clear water. It dried in less than a second—proof that the brick was at least centuries old. More bricks were uncovered; George and the crew dug with their bare hands. Every bit of clay found now was important for analysis to determine how the bricks had been used, and how they

64

had been made. Dr. Craig thought aloud: "A combination of sand, straw and mortar, no doubt." He shook his head. "Possibly remnants of a temple once used by nomads as they wandered through Cyprus. We'll soon know."

The charcoal brazier began to glow. They sat down to a shish-ke-bab supper, at an old bridge table that wobbled. Between bites, Kathy said, "Well, the ghost won't want those bricks. There are probably thousands inside that castle."

"Must be millions of bricks in that castle wall, under the cement covering," George said, thinking he must get the courage, and soon, to go back to the castle. The treasure could be no place else on the Island of Cyprus but there. There simply was no other hiding place. How could there be?

Sabri, the beggar from Nicosia came into the camp, crying out among the diggers who had been paid that day. "Alms! Alms!" The Turkish words had the smoothness of honey flowing from a spoon. Yet when the men didn't reach into their pockets quickly enough, Sabri fell to the ground, cursed them, and moaned, thoroughly enjoying himself, until the piasters fell at his feet.

Begging was an honest business, George thought, for a one-armed man.

6

>>>>>

A Tap-tap-tapping!

HAPPY THAT THIS WAS SATURDAY, GEORGE HAD ONLY three hours of work at the dig before he could go to see the new American movie at the Apollo. He dug into layers of earth on the south end of camp. Shortly before the coke break, Kathy hollered: "I've hit something."

When the hard earth was cleared away, they found a jar and worked with dental instruments when they felt several objects embedded inside it. Dr. Craig examined the find. "This is typical of the art work exported by the ancient Egyptians. Other jars like it have been found in Crete."

Inside the main tent, they removed the encrustrations from the smaller pieces and examined a remnant of a bronze necklace, four inches long; an earring in the shape of a bull's head; a solid gold coin used in the time of the Crusaders, two inches in diameter. The last object was so overlaid with crust it had to be soaked overnight in a specially prepared solution.

"All masterpieces of ancient craftsmanship." Dr. Craig couldn't be more pleased with their find. He left a sentry on duty.

Patting his rifle butt, the sentry said, with Turkish fire, "Let the thief—or ghost—come. I am ready."

In town, George bought a shish-ke-bab lunch out of his salary and later relaxed in the Apollo. It was his kind of movie, *Spartacus*. He saw it twice, and when he left the theatre it was dark. On the way home, the narrow streets were empty, and the shops closed. When alone like this, his imagination caused him to hear the rattle of chains. Still he had not found the courage to return to the castle wall. He made himself more frightened by nervously repeating the verse that Kathy had taught him last week from *The Rime of the Ancient Mariner*:

Like one, that on a lonesome road
Doth walk in fear and dread,
And having once turned round walks on,
And turns no more his head;
Because he knows a fearful fiend
Doth close behind him tread.

When he did reach home, he was so happy to find Ajax completely well, he forgot the ghost, and the castle wall. At 9:30, George went to bed on his cot beneath the shutter in the living room —a shutter tightly closed at night to keep away germs that the night air brought. Sleep came quickly, following a day of work and play.

George had no idea how long he had been asleep when something woke him. Everything was in darkness, a darkness that shaped itself from the mist. A pale, weary, flickering light came from the crack in the closed shutter. A flame without heat. A ghost of a flame. George lay without moving, and although the night was hot, he shivered so hard he might easily step out of his skin.

The church bell tolled the hour of twelve when a tap-tap-tap sounded on the closed shutter.

69

George stiffened. It might be a crow that had eaten fermented fruit, gotten drunk, and had stumbled against the shutter causing those tap-tap-tapping sounds. The ghost? He tried to call out but no sound came. And, if he were mistaken and it was only a bird out there, his father would be angry with him again for disturbing his rest. Yet fear gnawed at him like a rat he couldn't kick away, as the tap-tap-tapping continued against the shutter and against his nerves.

George pulled the sheet over his head, realizing that the shutter was tightly locked, and that no one could get into the room. Yet his nerves became like hot wires as the tapping kept on and on into the night. The bright moon cast a shadow through the crack in the shutter. When he couldn't breathe under the sheet, he stuck out his head to stare at a shadow that resembled a giant crab with claws that clung to the wall like fungus. A hand! A hand that tapped-tapped-tapped. Ghost or no ghost, George had to know.

Softly and silently he crept to the shutter lock, then yanked it open. Something brushed his hand, stabbed at his knuckles and tore the skin. A voice insisted: "Forget the golden-winged horse."

Claw-like hands tore at his tee shirt until it pulled apart like paper. The ghost was now so close George couldn't blink without touching him. His chest might burst with fright. He no longer had a heart, but a hammer that pounded against his ribs like a wild hare. His breathing was short and rapid as leaf-shadows fell across the skull-face, giving it a sick half-grin, a one-eyed leer. In the still night air, the ghost made hissing noises.

Suddenly, George struck out in terror and clutched the ghost-face with both hands; it felt as round and puffy as a cold dumpling. Still he couldn't let go, but hung on in sheer fright, blinking several times as if this were a nightmare and blinking would wake him up. Then—all that was left of the ghost was the skull that George held in his hands. He yelled for all he was worth!

His father ran into the room, demanding, "Why are you yelling?"

George stammered out what had happened and, in a flash, his father went through the open shutter to search for the intruder, yelling so loudly himself that he soon had the other villagers searching and yelling with him. When the panic ended long past dawn, they had found no sign of a ghost, nor a single clue, other than the skull-mask left behind by the stranger.

Sunday proved more pleasant. George took Kathy to visit his grandmother, and they carried candles, a basket of dried fish, and a broken oar which George slung over his shoulder. Yaryar, his grandmother, used this as a shovel to bring bread from the large outdoor oven. It was a long, hot walk to Yarosha Village, made heavy by the oar, and annoying by the hoards of flies. "This dust has teeth."

Kathy couldn't agree more. "I'm almost spitting sand."

At the crossroads, in front of the coffee shop, schoolmates, sitting idle on the steps, taunted George. "Hello, hello, how is the ghost-catcher?"

It was too hot to lose one's temper. George ignored them, which made the boys all the more angry.

"Hey, you, George Logo, with such great courage, how come you spend all your time with a girl, eh?"

"Eh? Eh?" the others chorused.

"You insult my friend," he shouted, swinging the oar at their heads until they scattered like

73

pigeons. "She's not a girl, but almost an archae-ologist."

Kathy, quite pleased with the compliment, helped George carry the oar. Both were relieved to reach the arbor where copious grapes hung like wall carpets outside his grandmother's cottage. Yaryar had a pitcher of cold water waiting, along with Turkish Delight sweets.

George introduced Kathy, hooking his fingers in the armpits of his patched shirt as grown men do when they are very proud. "Yaryar, my turtle dove, this is my friend Kathy. There is much love in my heart for her. She is my friend."

Yaryar looked closely at Kathy, then said that her nose was too long for a Greek's, too short for a Turk's. And that she had never seen such long, straight, strong legs on a girl before.

"I am an American," Kathy said, proudly.

Yaryar had white hair tied into a bun at the top of her head, beautiful eyes, skin as brown as a dry leaf, and not a single tooth.

Kathy entertained her by mimicking a dove, mockingbird, cricket, and donkey, as the woman laughed joyously, and later hugged Kathy to her bosom, asking the name of her village in America.

"Philadelphia," Kathy answered, and Yaryar

74

was indeed pleased that there were Greek-named cities in the United States. Kathy answered questions about her family's wealth: they were not rich or influential, but average middle-class Americans—happy and relaxed because they were real "gung ho" about their own personal freedom, as well as the individual beliefs of every person.

"As Dad says, if you jump off a diving board into a waterless pool, you're going to learn in person that you'll get an awful headache."

George complained. "Here we must do every little thing our parents tell us. But," he shrugged, "now that I have learned to read, my parents let me do some things without asking first." He grinned, "Remember, kiddo, that ancient Greece gave the world the idea of freedom."

"And we Americans knew how to put the ideal to work."

Yaryar wanted to hear more about Kathy's "village of Phil-a-del-phi-a" and Kathy explained about its museums, schools, libraries and that it is called "the city of brotherly love."

Yaryar was astonished at the number of people in Kathy's city. How was it possible to say "good morning" and "good night" to each one? She shook her head slowly at the wonderment of

it all: a city larger than her own entire country!

Later, as a baby goat nibbled bits of grass from Yaryar's palm, she told how she had not been able this year to sew new shirts for George, but instead had mended and patched his old ones as she sat in the arbor each day. Yaryar, blessed with a happy nature, believed that next year would be a giant olive year. "Ah, then, money enough for everything."

Soon they got around to talking about the ghost of the fifth door. The tiny goat with ringing bells leaped and wound itself, like a puppy, around Kathy's legs as she begged for the story.

George translated as his grandmother told, in solemn tones, the legend of the ghost of the fifth door. She told them how Cyprus, until it had recently become a republic, had been ruled by many conquerors: Romans; Ottoman Turks; Venetians; and lastly, the British. Legends, therefore, were as plentiful as grapes on the Island and one had one's pick of superstitions that had been handed down for centuries by word of mouth.

"Turtle dove, tell us the legend about the ghost."

"A story is told of a knight, once bold and true,

who had taken part in many crusades. Then, wounded in battle, he entered the Castle of Kyrenia in the time of Richard the Lionhearted, and he was to live there as a hermit in one of the dungeons. Four others followed, Crusaders all; when they died many years later, their bodies were found. The hermit's body has never been found, yet his ghost has been seen in many shapes and forms through the years . . ."

"Is there a way of opening the fifth door in the castle wall?" George asked, impatient to know more.

Yaryar remembered some talk of how four of the doors were permanently sealed, but the delta door was hollow; in the chamber beyond it were the skeletons dressed in armour that faced the fifth door where the spirit of the ghost rested, if and when he rested. "I can tell no more." To her, the mystery itself was more exciting than the solving of it. This ended, for the time being, all talk of the ghost and the castle wall.

George, prompted by his grandmother, asked, "Kiddo, do you have a yaryar?"

"Oh, yes, my grandmother's a retired school teacher in Ovid, New York. She's a volunteer, now, at the children's ward of the County Hospital."

Yaryar was astonished that a woman of her own years, and a grandmother, could read the insides of books—and that women could be schoolmasters in the United States.

George explained: "In Yaryar's time there was no schooling in Cyprus. Shepherds don't need books to tend their flocks and do the fish care if the fisherman can't read or write?" He moaned, "Now it is so different. All I hear is—study, study, study. Whew!" George wiped his brow.

"That computes," Kathy said. "I'm a charter member of that club."

When it was time to leave, Yaryar handed Kathy a mason jar of grape jam.

"She loves you," George said simply. "That is one of her best jars."

Kathy thanked Yaryar before they headed down the long road from the arbor, walking easier now without the oar and basket of fish.

Dr. Craig met Kathy at the coffeehouse crossroads and drove George to Kyrenia in the jeep, before he returned to the dig to write up another of those endless, routine reports that were a necessary part of his job.

George ran to the beach to greet his father who was mending a fishing net—a big toe hooked into the mesh, keeping it taut while he made repairs. The sharp sea air teased his eyes and nose; smacked against his ears, as if warning him not to move on toward trying to solve the mystery. The castle of fear, now a wall of eyes staring at him, defied him, George Logo, to test its power —to win or lose, again, the golden-winged horse.

7

>>>>>

George, the Brave

IT WAS MONDAY MORNING AND GEORGE, ON HIS WAY
to work, climbed the secret path. The air was
velvet-soft and smelled of lemon blossoms. Exhausted by wilting heat, he stopped to rest in the
dense orchard of orange and lemon trees beneath
the waterfall that was noisy with cascading water.
A jet zipped across the sky casting a shadow on a
farmer pushing an ox-drawn plow on the slope,
and on George, eagle-spread, relaxing in the
shade.

He peered down in the valley where a handful
of gypsies were pulling donkeys laden with pots,
blankets and shovels. A small girl guided a milk-

white camel, a rare sight in the Middle East. George thought, "I shall have good luck today, for having seen the albino." No more time to rest, he started the slippery climb, again, upward. The morning was soundless, except for the waterfall and the banana leaves that rattled like parchment, although there was no breeze. Carefully on the vertical ascent George secured a toehold and moved cautiously.

A sudden movement among the pomegranates startled him: a wild hare, no doubt, and no need to become nervous. Beyond the falls the arbor ended and the endless black tunnel through the Troodos mountain began. He would bypass this and head for the open spring.

Then, before he could turn away from the cave, he froze with fear. Inside the cave a ghost-white face commanded his attention, against his will, it seemed. The face, or mask, gaped through the mist until George shook in terror, and twisting and turning until his body was like a crooked stick, he stared back. Behind the ghost face was that same thin, pale, weary light that he had seen from the tip of the delta-shaped fifth door, and also through the shutter the night the ghost had visited his home.

There seemed to be no body; only the skull face was visible. Eyes like dried green olives stared from the skull, like a mad animal glaring through the bars of a cage. Realizing the danger he was in, George yelled louder than the cascading water, and, with legs like rubber, he shinnied up the boulder, clutching at an overhanging branch —but not soon enough.

The ghost caught his right ankle. George clasped a palm trunk until it stabbed his chest; still, he would not let go, even when he thought the ghost would yank off his foot. With his left foot he kicked hard, until the clutching fingers released him. Then he jumped up and raced to the dusty mountain road that cut through the orchard. He seemed to be all legs, scared legs that ran like a frightened rabbit, until, finally, he fell and buried his head in his hands as a heavy wheezing and clomp of feet behind him made him think that the ghost had followed. His bones felt as watery as the Mediterranean. Too scared to peek through his open fingers at that awful face, he heard the clomping come closer. Seconds passed and when nothing happened, George looked over his shoulder. A sheep! Greatly re-lieved, he gave the animal a good piece of his

mind for pretending to be a ghost, and didn't stop berating the sheep until he heard a cry for help —in Turkish.

The sounds came from the cave. Could it be a trap? Was the ghost trying to trick him? He listened closely. It was Char's voice. Char was in danger and needed help. But Char was his enemy. Would a Turk, these days, go to *his* aid? He decided to ignore the plea and go on to work.

But George couldn't leave. He ran to the cave and found Char on the ground with a large gash on his forehead, and unconscious. George rinsed the cut with spring water and stopped the bleeding by packing the cut with a clean, wet handkerchief. Then, certain that Char had no broken bones, he dragged him carefully up the slope and placed him in the shade of a tree.

A Turkish peasant from the field by the highway hurried over fingering amber beads to the ninety-nine names of Allah and blurted out: *"To moro, pos ine?"* (How is the boy?)

George answered in Greek, and the old man accused him of causing Char's accident, and waved a hoe threateningly at his head.

"Oki, oki, no, no, he is my friend," George insisted.

Now that he had said the word "friend" he knew he could never again refer to Char as enemy.

"Friend?" Char muttered as the cool water and the shade revived him. "George?"

George helped him to his feet. They walked together, slowly, until at long last, they reached the dig, where Dr. Craig listened to their story.

"On impulse," Char said, "I decided not to take the bus, but come the secret way, like George, and give the money I saved to my grandmother."

He had been hit on the head and dragged to the cave.

"One of you must have seen more than his face?" Dr. Craig asked, puzzled, "The clothes he was wearing?"

Char recalled nothing—only complete blackness and the ghost face. "There was no body," he said.

Dr. Craig let out his breath slowly, then whistled. "George, you're not one to let a fly pass by your nose, even on the hottest day. Surely, you looked down when he clutched your ankle?"

"*Oki*," George answered, shaking his head, no.

The mystery was heightened when the police reported that not a single clue, or scrap of evidence had been found in the cave; nor had anyone in the area seen a stranger in the vicinity.

"My theory is that the thief came up the secret path that the boys use," Dr. Craig said, "put on the trench coat when he stole the golden-winged horse. But how did he get away from here, and to the castle without being seen? It's uncanny. And where is he now? The castle wall has been searched." He could add nothing new to the puzzle.

Later George and Kathy sat under a pepper tree, sipping cokes. Char joined them and they talked of nothing but the ghost, even when they returned to work, and, after work, Kathy asked, truly worried, "Why don't you let Dad drive you home in the jeep?"

"We'll be okay, kiddo," George insisted.

Char added, "Kyrenia is out of the way. Your father has a dig report to write up—a long report."

Still nervous, she cautioned, "But the ghost might pop out at you, any time."

George swallowed hard. "He won't dare, kiddo, I'll swat him away like a fly." He was feeling brave; very brave. He reasoned that if he were the ghost he wouldn't go to the castle wall when the UN patrol was there. He waved so-long to Kathy and left for Kyrenia.

Dinner was pleasant, but very quiet: his father was thinking of fish that wouldn't bite; his mother was thinking—who knew what women thought about? George pretended to be very sleepy. He went to his cot and rested. Then, when his parents went to bed, he got up, and folded his pillow under the sheet, to look as if he were sleeping. Then, he crept out of the house.

Shortly before midnight George went to the left pier, adjacent to the castle, and onto the balcony of the yacht club. From there he threw a knotted rope over the edge and dropped to earth near a eucalyptus tree. With his back against its trunk he settled down to keep his vigil.

At midnight, there was the tolling of church bells, then complete silence once again. His legs were stiff from remaining crouched in the shade of the tree. Then, he heard a strange clicking noise. Where had he heard it before? George listened carefully, almost holding his breath.

A clicking of beads, but not the usual cadence of a Muslim's continual homage to Allah!

The longer the clicking continued, the more

familiar it became. Last Saturday at the market-place—the Arab who seemed an ordinary Arab and, yet, was peculiar in some way—had clicked his amber beads in the same manner. Now the sound came from the basin of the harbor where the fishing boats lay, overturned, with nets spread atop. A net was pulled from a boat, then from beneath the overturned boat emerged a figure, like someone rising from a coffin.

It was the ghost, only its bony skull head visible, and once again, no body. The head went toward the castle wall. George stood up, ready to follow at a safe distance, when a net was tossed over him. He was gagged, tied up like a trussed chicken, dragged along the beach and hung from a branch outside his own house. A message was pinned to the seat of his pants.

Char cut him down. "While you were watching for the ghost, I was watching for you."

He explained how he could not cross the green line that separated their villages because there had been a Greek partisan on vigilante patrol until only minutes before George had been hung on the branch.

"George, there are two of them."

"I know, because the ghost went to the castle

wall, at the same time someone trapped me."

"The ghost who carried you here had no skull head or mask. George, it was as if you were sailing along through the night, like a flying carpet."

"Hey, look," Char removed the note from the seat of George's pants, and George yelled when the pin stuck him.

The message read:

LAST WARNING TO GEORGE LOGO
THE NEXT TIME WE MEET WILL
BE YOUR LAST MOMENT ON EARTH

(Signed)
The Ghost of the Fifth Door

8

>->->->->-

A Clicking Noise

CHIEF INSPECTOR ARCH PAPANO TRAMPED EXCITED-
ly up and down the main tent, waving a black
umbrella and saying, "You were wise, Dr. Craig,
to call the world's greatest antiquities criminolo-
gist, namely, me."

"I read in the *Journal* of the American Schools
of Archaeology, Arch, that you had solved the
case of the Israeli smuggling ring."

"All is not solved, yet. That ring spreads like
a spiderweb throughout the Near and Middle
East." He tut-tutted a little. "It operates from
Piraeus to Haifa. The leader may be here in
Cyprus."

93

Papano barked a question at George: "When you removed this mask from his face that night at your shutter window, what did you see?" The Inspector held the ghost mask from the tip of his umbrella and waved it in front of George's nose.

George shook his head. "Nothing."

"Nothing?" Papano roared. "There is no such thing as nothing. Even when you put sugar in water it does not disappear. Taste it and it's still there. The thief has a body and a human face."

George shook his head again.

Papano groaned. "This boy has seen the thief at close range twice and he is bewitched into thinking it is a ghost." He slumped into a folding chair. "What we must find out is *how* the thief hides his body. This thief is clever enough to be the leader of the smuggling ring. Until I capture him, he is even smarter than I. This, I don't like." He blew his nose vigorously into a monogrammed handkerchief. "Now, a clever operator doesn't tie up a boy, hang him in a net and pin a message to his behind, unless he believes that you, George Logo, can identify him beyond doubt. Think back to the night that your uncle gave the golden-winged horse to you. There is someone on this

Island, who, when he is not playing the role of a ghost, is the thief, or his accomplice. You know who he is."

When the Inspector finally released him, George joined Kathy at the south site of the dig. "Wow, he's almost as scary as the ghost, kiddo."

"He's really nice. He just can't stand antiquities criminals."

Hagob, the Armenian, drove into camp and parked the jeep in the north enclosure. Mrs. Craig was with him, sitting in the back, where chickens, tied in bunches like vegetables, squawked. George helped her out of the jeep, then lit the brazier for Hagob. They would all share a shish-ke-bab lunch.

During lunch, Papano said, through tightened lips, "I must plan a trap for this ghost-thief." He looked at George as if he were to be part of the bait.

"Arch, he may know you're here. There are no secrets in Cyprus."

Mrs. Craig added, "I've never heard of a more clever thief."

The Inspector wiped his lips daintily. "My dear, giving the devil his due, when I think of all the criminals that I have known, most of them

96

were more fool than clever. They almost always trap themselves, sooner or later."

"I hope this one will be sooner," Dr. Craig admitted. "I spend hours each day writing back to the Foundation, instead of working. I received a cable yesterday that simply said there will be no more checks until the relic is recovered."

This was serious! George let out a slow whistle. No one could continue working after tomorrow's paycheck. Char was trying to hide his fear. As it was, he and his grandmother would eat nothing during the coming year except cheap Cyprus beans, George knew. He must ask Ba-ba to give him some fresh fish for Char. It was difficult for the Turkish minority on Cyprus since the hostility; some of their villages were cut off completely from the outside world, and most could work only for friendly foreigners, like Dr. Craig.

George would have to do something; and no later than tonight. He thought hard, then, after his evening meal, he slipped out of the house, wrapped in an old black shawl of his mother's, to meet Char and Kathy. In his path he found a dead bird, the mouth stiffly open, the eyes glassy, blood on the wing. George buried it. And, as the sun dipped toward twilight, he passed through

97

the silent street like a shadow. From the sea the castle looked anchored to the cliff, overshadowed by the mountain of Troodos.

They met as agreed, on the road beyond the cliff that led to the Abbey of Bellas Pais. The three of them passed through the outer line of trees and went into the garden of the Abbey. Not a sound could be heard anywhere. Far below the cliff, forming a short, slender line in the belly of the valley, were a few scattered cement houses. George, followed by Kathy and Char, tiptoed silently past a catacomb. A bright moon through the iron bars showed the neat stacks of bones and rows of skulls, all with small black identifying numbers on the foreheads.

Positive that no one could overhear them, George told of his plan. "We can get the golden-winged horse and the reward money."

"And save our jobs for the summer," Char added, gravely.

George took the message that the ghost had pinned to his shorts from his shirt pocket, and handed it to Kathy, advising, "Turn it over."

"International Morse Code?" she asked.

"No," Char said. "That's what George and I first thought. But if it were straight International

Morse Code, the police could crack it immediately, so the thieves used another trick. We worked on it all night," Char added, "and found that it's a modified code. It has fourteen letters —dots, dashes and spaces."

"This has dots and dashes."

"Look," Char pointed out, "SOS should be ... — — — ..., *this code is different.* We figured from this small sample that one dot means *S*, two dots, *E*, and one dash is *N* or *M*—and when we broke the code, it read:

Craig sending for Papano. Take care!

"This is what the Inspector meant when he said that a criminal traps himself sooner or later. When the thief wrote this message he grabbed the first piece of paper he could find without knowing that his own secret code was on the back," George explained, then continued, "When that fake Arab clicks those amber beads he's sending secret messages to an accomplice. Now that we know the code, it will lead us to the golden-winged horse."

9

>>>>>

To the Castle!

DAYS LATER, ON FRIDAY NIGHT, THE BOYS RETURNED to the beach.

Because of the danger, George and Char decided to explore the castle wall without Kathy. Making certain that his parents were sleeping soundly, George slipped out of the house, tied a knot in the rope around his khaki shorts, and placed the rest of it over his shoulder. There was no movement in the air, no sound save the sea against rock, and no light except a faint kerosene lamp here and there in the village, and a new moon with a cloudy ring around it.

George closed the garden gate securely; now Ajax could not follow him to the medieval castle. Walking on, he found the night filled with inky shadows, darker than a tomb, and became shaky when he remembered the message he had received from the ghost-thief. And, at the meeting place, when Char whispered, "Hi," George leaped into the air like a cat.

The boys crept down the crooked steps that led to the beach, then to the pier. They ran soundlessly through the white sand, crawled onto the boulder, facing the castle wall. The place was deserted: nothing could be seen or heard. Moving up the slippery rocks that resembled a ladder of coal, George pointed out the pitfalls. "That rock shaped like an arrowhead, watch it, it wobbles."

Char lassoed the heavy rope around an iron ring on the parapet of the castle wall and hoisted himself up. George followed. They circled the entire wall by crawling along the parapet.

When they paused to rest, George whispered, "Listen for a clicking noise."

When an hour of listening passed, they had heard nothing. Char said, "Let's go in opposite directions." There was a Turkish saying that what you often cannot find with the left eye is sometimes found with the right.

A scratching noise against the rocks below made George freeze. Someone was climbing onto the parapet, using the rope they had left for a quick escape, if they ran into trouble. Almost too scared to turn around, he called, "Char?" But, his friend was in plain sight on the opposite wall.

"George Logo, you sneak," someone called.

"Kathy, what are you doing here?"

"I thought you might try something like this. From the balcony of my friend Urania's house, I saw you and Char climb this wall."

"This is no place for a girl," he warned.

"Remember—I'm almost an archaeologist. Three of us are better than two, to try to find the secret entrance. At dinner I heard Dad say that Inspector Papano has a police boat close by in the harbor. It's disguised as a fishing boat. They watch this wall around the clock."

Char hurried over, complaining. "You are making enough noise to raise the dead."

Suddenly, there was a flash of what seemed to be lightning, or a strong beam from the harbor, and it struck the northwest side of the wall facing the Mediterranean. George never knew what hit

him, but one instant he was on the parapet; the next, in the sea. He could see nothing; he swam in blue-black shadows, on the south side of the castle wall, completely out of sight of the harbor and the yacht club. Nothing was familiar. This frightened him.

Exhausted, he dragged himself against a turret and, gasping, hung by his fingers to a rusted iron ring. It was so dark, he couldn't see his palm in front of his face. Too weary to panic, he rested against the wall. "Char? Kathy?" he shouted, worried about his friends.

"Use a strong torch, we'll find him yet," a hoary voice yelled, then another answered, "Stupid— the light that would reveal him to us would also show us to the police that are out there, if the American girl is right."

Again, complete silence.

As if in a dream, George saw a square yellow rock tilt out from the castle wall, looking like a lower casement that had been built in, several feet above the sea. What moved it? he wondered. The rock crevice crept open, slowly. Waist-deep in water, he waded to the opening, less frightened since he had not heard another sound from the hoary voices. He clutched at the ledge until it was at eye level; then he looked inside.

"Hi, George!" Kathy and Char both greeted him.

"What on earth?" George was amazed.

"After you fell into the sea, we searched for you. Char saw this yellow square. We climbed down the wall and hid in here when we heard the thieves shouting at one another."

A beam of light threw its glare against the wall. The police boat? There was no use calling for help; in the strong sea wind it was difficult to be heard at any distance. And, this would be their first, perhaps last, chance to go inside the castle. George had waited for this opportunity for as long as he could remember, and since the thieves had taken off, the danger was gone. From the thieves, yes; from the ghost, no.

"We've gone too far to turn back now," Kathy said.

Yet, inside, they felt uneasy when the rock window shut tightly behind them. George stood in a dry moat. The drawbridge over the moat had been reversed; instead of leading to and from the castle, it had been cut down to scale and now led into the castle wall. This was how the Venetians had gotten their treasures to the ships.

When the wind blew it was as if voices could

be heard from the ancient past, ordering their seamen to hurry with the loading, so they could set sail for Italy.

Beyond the wall, the castle itself resembled a mountainous mailed fist. Every crevice and entrance and exit had been permanently sealed with cement; it was impossible to even imagine anything as gloomy as the sealed castle.

"Reminds me of the witch scene in *Snow White*," Kathy whispered, her knees knocking together.

When they approached the leeward side of the wall, chains rattled. This was the sound of the death dance George had heard from the parapet the night that he had found the trench coat. The chains were the only way of going up the drawbridge from the door in the wall. The loose, heavy, rusted chains rattled from the sea breeze.

"We must climb up the chain," Char said, "so the drawbridge will open under our weight."

Kathy called out, "One-two-three-a-go-go," and they shinnied up the chain, until the drawbridge parted and they could slip inside, then down another rusty chain that sounded even more like a death dance than the outside chain.

George was the first to lower himself. He stood

on solid ground and endless bats started up like a storm. His two friends followed. When their eyes adjusted to the dark, they found themselves in a room about 24 by 18 feet, with an earth floor, as dry as if tiled. The walls were covered with so many bats they ran like wallpaper down the thirty foot height. A slit, ten feet above the floor, admitted a little moonlight that cast a pale yellow gloom. Sea wind moaned along the wall, but there was hardly any air in the room.

"I can't stand these bats," Kathy cried.

"I could stand seeing the ghost more easily," Char agreed.

George had seen bats before, but never as many as this.

They kept their hands waving above their heads until Char found a burned candle, and next to it, a dry match. "When I light this, the bats will keep away."

With the lighted wick they could see a rat nibbling some leftover food in a corner. "The thieves must have been living in here."

Fastened to a bolt and hanging against the north wall were a pair of heavy chains, thick with rust that stained the wall. Holding the candle tightly, George stumbled across a case of canned food, and next to this, a barrel of dirty water.

Kathy screeched when she tripped over a skull. Loose dust poured down from the ceiling in a steady stream and made their noses itch; the carbon of antiquity was everywhere. Char's big toe hit against the skull that Kathy had tripped over.

Then, as the candle gave up a final flick of light, they saw everything that was to be seen in the fifth door of the wall: supported by iron rings attached to the wall, four skeletons shook within their armour, looking as if it had been put on only that morning. The skeletons faced a sarcophagus and on this, his head resting on his shield, was the ghostly knight of the fifth door. His right hand clasped a giant sword, his chain mail was covered with a surcoat, and on this, a large, faded blue cross—the sign of a Crusader.

"Knights are very nice to ladies," George whispered. "You go take a closer look, Kathy."

She ran her hands over the face of bronze and found it strong and handsome. Surely the statue had been done by one of the world's finest sculptors. George and Char took a closer look, then went back to the barrel.

George put his hand into the barrel, to wash the dust from his face. "Kathy, Char," he whispered. "Look at this!" He dragged out a black skindiving suit.

Char fished around with his long arms and came up with the head gear: a rubber skull. He slipped it over his head.

"Ug," Kathy screeched. "That's enough to scare anybody. Please take it off." She stepped back against the wall, and let out another scream. "There's a snake on my foot."

George leaned over. "No, it's those amber beads."

"Look!" Char pointed. "Arab clothes."

They had all made some startling discoveries.

10

>>>>>

A Feast

GEORGE, CHAR AND KATHY MADE A DASH FOR THE rusty chain of the drawbridge. Their combined weight broke the chain; now they could leave the castle at will.

"I hear footsteps," Char whispered.

The drawbridge descended slowly, like a freight elevator. George, Kathy and Char crouched in a dark corner, fearful that the noise might have aroused the thieves. But it wasn't the thieves. Inspector Papano, followed by a squad of Cypriot police, both Greek and Turk, shouted: "Hands up, hands up, or we shoot."

"It's only us," Kathy called.

The police held torches above their heads until

the room was as bright as a ballroom. The Inspector demanded: "What are you doing here? It's against the law to enter this castle."

George and Char were still shaking in the corner, but Kathy faced the Inspector and explained: "We came in here to escape the thieves. And—we found many clues for you."

The Inspector commanded the boys to come out of the corner. "Stand on unshaking feet and tell us what you know."

"First," George said, "we found these hidden in a rain barrel." He presented the black rubber skin-diving suits, complete with head covering to the Inspector.

"So, that's how they hid their bodies against the darkness of night and in the cave.

"What else?" he asked, standing on tiptoe until he was as tall as George and Char.

"They dress as Arabs, and when they click their beads, they are not praising Allah, but sending secret messages." Char explained the code to Inspector Papano.

"You young people have done fine detective work, you shall be rewarded," the Inspector promised.

Kathy said, sadly, "We did not find the golden-winged horse."

"The scoundrels would keep that with them at all times." Papano ordered the squad of police to question the few Arabs in Nicosia. Any who did not know the ninety-nine names of Allah were to be arrested. "There will be only two in all Cyprus who do not know, and those are the ones we want."

Char asked Dr. Craig. "The ghost light, what caused it?"

"That's easy to answer, fella."

The flame without heat, the ghost of a flame, was methane gas, used continuously by explorers, archaeologists, and those who work underground, like coal miners.

Thus, the mystery of the ghost of the fifth door was solved and the ghost laid to rest for all time. But, the golden-winged horse must be found.

The fake Arabs were soon caught and brought to headquarters. George identified the tall, thin Arab with a beard like a goat, and a smell to match, as the one who had threatened him the night Uncle Spiros gave the antiquity to him. He was also the Arab George had seen in the marketplace that Saturday, staring at him.

Neither man would say a word about the golden-winged horse, and after they were thoroughly searched, they were allowed to keep the amber beads, and George was posted within hearing distance of their cells, to learn the whereabouts of the relic, when they did communicate. George stretched out on the hard bench in the corridor, and folded his arms under his head for comfort. He waited. After hours of waiting, the convicts still did not try to communicate with each other, and George, impatient with the passing of time, tried to think where he, if he had to, would have hidden the treasure. When the idea came to him, he jumped up and ran out into the night.

At the dusty crossroads he scattered chickens out of his way, turned to his right and took the path along the edge of the cliff. There was a full moon and the sky so full of stars that they could be read by. He made his way quickly to the village of St. George, then beyond the lemon tree avenue, he entered the house of his late uncle, Spiros.

He unscrewed the solid wood that seemed a part of the bed, then tugged at the black, red, and yellow threads of the protecting cloth. There it was! The golden-winged horse.

"You see," George told Inspector Papano, "they

117

knew that Uncle Spiros had safely hidden the treasure in his house for over twenty years. No one would think of searching the house, but only the castle."

"No one but you." The Inspector couldn't praise George enough.

The village of Kyrenia marveled in joy at the bravery of one of their finest young men, George Logo. They gave credit, as well to Char and Kathy. There would be a great feast to honor all the young people: Char's village, and the American colony of archaeologists were invited to eat all that they could hold of hot wheat bread, feta and other cheeses, thick charcoal-broiled lamb chops, endless varieties of Cyprus salads, and juicy melons called peponi.

Mr. and Mrs. Logo contributed a delicious suckling pig crisply roasted on a spit. Mr. Logo, beaming with fatherly pride, shouted, "Enjoy!" He waved his arms. "Everyone enjoy the good food."

Mrs. Logo and her friends had spent days making homemade sausage, and rice and meat wrapped in vine leaves. With long poles, George

118

and Kathy had hit the olives loose from the trees and put them into the salad.

On tablecloths as white as pot cheese on the wooden tables in the arbor were pastries and cakes smothered with whipped cream and sliced fruit. It was a beautiful feast held under a bright blue cloudless sky in the garden that overlooked the crystal clear water of Kyrenia Harbor and the castle.

"Are you enjoying yourself, Yaryar, my turtle dove?" George asked his grandmother, who played Greek music on goats' bells for the guests.

"Could a grandmother, blessed with age, be more happy than to have a grandson named George Logo?"

Friends came from the village of Ledra and brought musicians who played lively music at the feast. Inspector Papano and Dr. Craig were very happy. "Since I could not be born tall," the Inspector confided, "I promised myself that I'd become famous." He strutted around the arbor. "Every newspaper in the world has told the story of how the great treasure was recovered and the smuggling ring squashed by Archimedes Odysseus Papano, the great one."

He blew his nose vigorously, then with a new

handkerchief from another pocket, wiped the tears from his eyes, saying to George and Char, "When the time comes, you will both go abroad to study archaeology. I have made arrangements."

"No one is on trial anymore," Dr. Craig told the boys. "You will both work all summer, and with a raise as of tomorrow. Also," he waved a cable that he had received from his Foundation that morning, "I can promise you work for many future summers."

George and Char stood at attention as Dr. Craig counted out one thousand piasters. He placed five hundred in one pile and five hundred in another. Seeing so much money at one time made George's head swim.

Char escorted his grandmother to the table and poured the money into her apron pocket. The piasters were so heavy, she took off her apron, and Char carried the money over his shoulder, like a pack.

Kathy did her bird imitations for the group, then, Ahmed, the foreman of diggers, fat as an elephant, did a toe dance and sang, "I'm as dainty as a mouse," until everyone held their sides with laughter.

The summer, like the feast, couldn't have been

a happier one, but it ended too quickly. All too quickly.

On September 10 the Craigs must fly home.

Saying goodbye at the airport terminal, George felt sad. "Here," he handed Kathy a basket filled with fine lace and dried fruit. "Yaryar put in three whole jars of jam. Her very best. She loves you very much."

Char handed Kathy a knitted shawl that his grandmother had made for her. "My grandmother loves you, too."

Kathy was so close to tears, she forgot, as she kissed them both, that she was almost an archaeologist.

"Well, old-timers," Dr. Craig said, shaking hands. "I'm glad you'll be working with me next summer."

"Wish you both were coming to the States." Kathy wiped the tears from her eyes with the sleeve of her blouse.

"I belong to Cyprus," George said. "I walk down the road and everyone I meet says to me 'hello.' I love my country as you love yours."

Char agreed. "I will someday go to Mecca as a good Muslim must, but I will return home to Cyprus, my country."

Kathy nodded, feeling as if her heart were made of marshmallow.

"So long, kiddo," George saluted, before he ambled away like a western cowboy.

The roar of the plane being revved up sounded more final than all their goodbyes put together. As the Craigs entered the aircraft, Char held up his hand.

"Say hello to everyone in the U.S. for me," George called.

When the plane touched the sky, heading west, out of sight, George and Char put their arms around each other's shoulders.

Both waiting for a new tomorrow!

The Author

Mary D. Roberts was born in Brooklyn, New York, in 1925. She was brought up by an Irish grandmother who had nine first names because, she claimed, nine fairy godmothers were present at her christening. Her other grandmother, as well as her Scotch-Irish grandfather, encouraged her to write, and daily fed her imagination with stories of the "old" and "new" country.

Educated at New York University and the University of the Americas (a Texas college in Mexico), she served in the WAC in World War II.

Mrs. Roberts has lived and traveled in many of the countries of Europe, the Mediterranean, the Middle and Near East, the Virgin Islands and most of the United States and Mexico. She lives in central Florida, is partially blind and takes special interest in visually handicapped children and in American Indian children. She has one daughter.